THE MAGICIAN'S VISIT

A PASSOVER TALE

adapted from a story by **I. L. Peretz**   retold by **Barbara Diamond Goldin**

illustrated by **Robert Andrew Parker**

VIKING

Special thanks to Professor David G. Roskies of the Jewish Theological
Seminary, who read this text for background authenticity.

The illustrations are hand-colored etchings and aquatint.

VIKING
Published by the Penguin Group
Penguin Books USA Inc., 375 Hudson Street, New York, New York 10014, U.S.A.
Penguin Books Ltd, 27 Wrights Lane, London W8 5TZ, England
Penguin Books Australia Ltd, Ringwood, Victoria, Australia
Penguin Books Canada Ltd, 10 Alcorn Avenue, Toronto, Ontario, Canada M4V 3B2
Penguin Books (N.Z.) Ltd, 182–190 Wairau Road, Auckland 10, New Zealand
Penguin Books Ltd, Registered Offices: Harmondsworth, Middlesex, England
First published in 1993 by Viking, a division of Penguin Books USA Inc.

10 9 8 7 6 5 4 3 2 1

Library of Congress Cataloging-in-Publication Data
Goldin, Barbara Diamond.
The magician's visit : a passover tale / Barbara Diamond Goldin:
illustrated by Robert Andrew Parker. p.   cm.
Summary: A poor Jewish couple is rewarded for their faith and charity by
a mysterious magician.
ISBN 0-670-84840-9
[1. Passover—Fiction.   2. Jews—Fiction.]   I. Parker, Robert Andrew, ill.   II. Title.
PZ7.G5674Mag   1993   [E]—dc20   92-22903 CIP AC

Printed in Hong Kong
Set in 15 pt. Pegasus

A magician came to town. It was the busy days before Passover and people were cleaning, washing, cooking, shopping. They would have walked right by any other magician, or violin player, or jokester. Yet they could not help but stop and notice this one.

He was a wonder. A man in rags who could pull yards and yards of fancy ribbons from his mouth. A half-starved figure who found turkeys as big as bears in his boots. Though he hadn't enough pennies to pay the innkeeper, the magician could nevertheless strike his shoe and bring forth rivers of gold coins.

The townspeople crowded around the magician. "Where are you from?" they asked.

"From Paris."

"Where are you going?"

"To London."

"How did you get here?"

"I wandered here," the magician answered one last time, and then vanished as though the earth had swallowed him, only to reappear on the other side of the marketplace. The magician left the townspeople's questions hanging in the air.

In this town lived a poor couple, Hayim-Jonah and
Rivkah-Bailah. Hayim-Jonah had once been a prosperous
lumberman but, through misfortune, had become
penniless. He and Rivkah-Bailah had just spent a winter
the likes of which they would not wish on even their
worst enemy. Here it was the Passover holiday, and they
had no money to buy the matzah and the wine, the herbs
and the food, for the Seder.

Hayim-Jonah would not borrow money from the loan society. He was a man of great faith.

"God will come to our aid," he said.

He gave what few pennies they had to the poor people's Passover fund, for he was a man of charity.

"There are others with less than we have," he said.

On Passover eve, Hayim-Jonah walked home from the synagogue. In all the windows of the houses he passed, candles glowed on the tables and glasses of wine sparkled before each place. His house alone was dark. Yet he did not feel discouraged.

"If God wills it, we will still have a good Passover," he said.

As he entered his house, he called "Happy holiday" to Rivkah-Bailah.

"Happy holiday," she replied sadly.

"Don't you know what day this is?" he asked her. "We celebrate our freedom today. No tears. If God has not chosen to let us have our own Seder, then we will go to a neighbor's. Everyone's door is opened on Passover. Come, put on your shawl."

At that moment, someone called, "Happy holiday."

"Happy holiday to you," Hayim-Jonah and Rivkah-Bailah replied, though they could not see the stranger's face in the dark.

"I would like to be a guest at your Seder."

"I'm sorry," said Hayim-Jonah, "but we have no Seder."

"No worry. I have brought the Seder with me," said the visitor.

15

"But we can't have the Seder in the dark," blurted out Rivkah-Bailah.

"Certainly not," said the visitor. There was a sound like the snapping of fingers, and two golden candlesticks with glowing candles danced in the air. In their light, Hayim-Jonah and Rivkah-Bailah saw the face of the stranger, the magician.

17

While they stared in wonder and fear, the magician turned to the table and said, "Come here and be spread with fine linen."

As soon as the magician's words were spoken, the table danced to the center of the room and a snowy white tablecloth dropped from the ceiling to cover it. The candlesticks landed safely on the cloth.

19

"Now we need couches," said the magician.

With the magician's words, three chairs sailed through the air to three sides of the table.

"Grow wider," said the magician.

They grew wider into large armchairs.

"Grow softer," he said.

And they were padded with red velvet. Pillows floated from the ceiling onto the chairs.

Another command, and a Seder plate with bitter
herbs, shankbone, greens, egg, and *haroset* appeared on
the table. Glasses of wine, matzah, and all things needed
for the feast followed.

"Do you have water for the washing?" asked the
magician. "If not, I can order that, too."

23

On hearing his question, Hayim-Jonah and Rivkah-Bailah came to life.

"Can we touch these things?" Rivkah-Bailah whispered to her husband.

"I don't know," Hayim-Jonah replied.

"You'd better go ask the Rabbi," she said.

"I can't let you stay here by yourself with the magician. We'll both go."

Leaving the magician alone with the feast, the two set off to see the Rabbi.

The Rabbi listened carefully to Hayim-Jonah and Rivkah-Bailah tell their story.

"What a magician produces is a deception, an illusion," the Rabbi said. "If you can crumble the matzah and pour the wine, if the pillows are soft to the touch, then you will know this is all a gift from Heaven."

27

They touched the matzah. It crumbled. They tipped the wine pitcher. The wine poured. They sat on the velvet chairs and sighed. So soft.

They understood then. Their Passover feast was a gift from Heaven, brought by the prophet Elijah himself.

ABOUT THIS BOOK

The eight-day spring holiday of Passover, also called the Feast of Freedom, commemorates the Israelites' exodus from ancient Egypt. Under the leadership of Moses, they left slavery to journey through the desert and become a nation.

Through the ages, Jews have relived the Israelites' journey by participating in the special ceremony called the *Seder*, traditionally held on the first two nights of the holiday. These evenings are filled with rituals, blessings, singing and telling, as well as a festive meal.

One of the rituals at the *Seder* includes placing a full cup of wine on the table for the Prophet Elijah. Later on during the ceremony, the door is opened for the Prophet. He is invited in with the hope that his arrival will herald the age of peace. In these ways, Elijah is very connected to the Passover holiday.

The Biblical Elijah lived in ancient Israel during the reign of King Ahab in the ninth century B.C.E. He was a zealous prophet who fought against the worship of the Semitic weather god Baal and for the worship of the one God.

According to Kings II, Elijah did not die, but was carried to heaven in a chariot of fire. During the centuries that followed, many stories arose about Elijah's reappearance on earth to help the poor and teach the scholars. Elijah became a folk hero and a symbol of hope for Jews of all countries.

Today, it is still customary to set aside a chair for Elijah at the circumcision of a baby boy, eight days after the child's birth. And at the end of the Sabbath, it is the custom to invoke Elijah's blessing for the new week.

In his story, "The Magician," written in 1904, I. L. Peretz tells how Elijah, in the guise of a magician, comes to the aid of a poor and pious couple at the time of the Passover Seder. Peretz chose him from all the heroes of the Bible, because Elijah belongs to every Jew, rich or poor, learned or simple, male or female.

I. L. Peretz lived in Poland from 1852 to 1915. He is one of the founders of modern Yiddish literature and a master of many literary forms: short stories, poems, plays, essays and memoirs. He was among the first Jewish writers to collect and rework Yiddish folktales and love songs and to be inspired by the teachings of the early Hasidic masters. His story, "The Magician," is rich in the details of Eastern European life and is rooted in the folk tradition of Elijah tales.